I'm Right Here

Written by
Constance Ørbeck-Nilssen

Illustrated by
Akin Duzakin

Eerdmans Books for Young Readers

Grand Rapids, Michigan • Cambridge, U.K.

"Are you ever afraid?" William asks Grandma.

"Sometimes, William," says Grandma. "Sometimes I'm afraid."
She stops and wipes away some sweat before taking a firm grip on
her cane again.

"What are you afraid of, then?" asks William.

Grandma looks up at the huge oak tree.

"That I won't see the squirrels anymore, William. I'm afraid of never seeing that cute squirrel again."

"But you see it every year," says William. "What else, Grandma? I mean something you're *really* afraid of."

Grandma leans on her cane and looks at William.

"That I won't see the white flowers in bloom — I'm afraid of never again seeing beautiful blossoms along our path."

"I'm afraid of angry dogs," says William.
"Stuff like that. That's the kind of thing I mean."

"I'm afraid that I won't hear the birds singing in the trees, my boy," says Grandma, "and be able to listen to their lovely twittering in the springtime."

"I'm afraid of stinging wasps," says William,
"and dangerous fires."

"I'm afraid that I won't see the swans down in the pond," says Grandma. "I'm afraid of never again seeing those proud white birds gliding across the water."

"I'm afraid of war," says William.
"I'm afraid at night, too, when it's so dark."

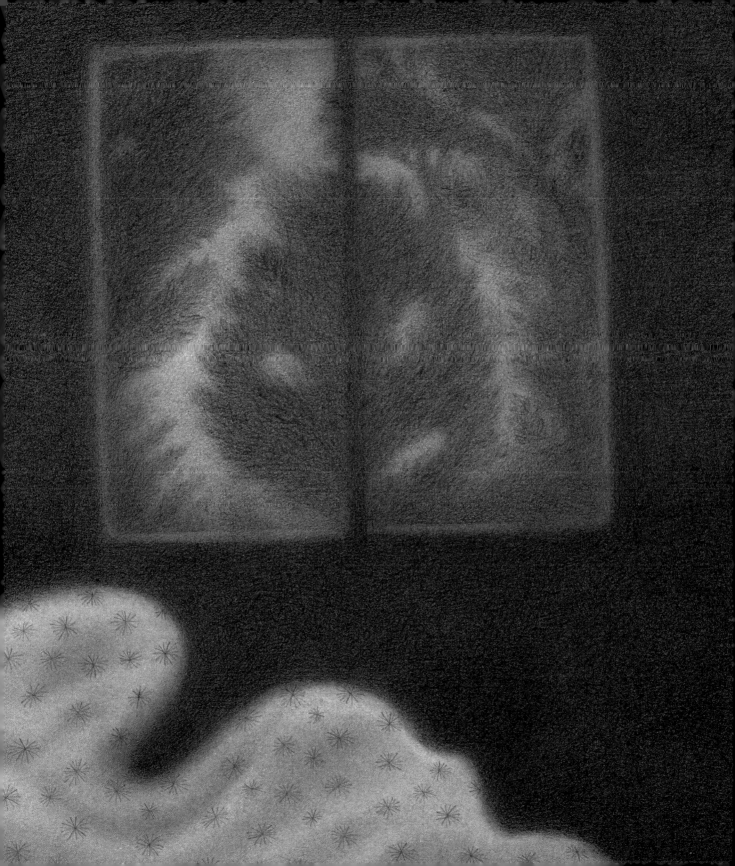

Grandma sits down. She has to rest her legs.

"And the magpie building its nest without my knowing it. That kind of thing," says Grandma. "That's what I'm afraid I won't get to see."

William sits down close to Grandma and waits for her to go on. But she leans her head back and shuts her eyes.

"Listen to me, Grandma. I'm afraid of big waves
and sharks and thunder and lightning," William goes
on, stretching his hand out to Grandma. "That's what
I mean. Not the things you're talking about."

Grandma opens her eyes and puts her arms around William.

"When I was little, I was afraid of nearly everything."

"Were you?" says William.

"Yes. But now that I'm old, I'm just afraid of losing everything I love. That's the kind of thing I think about."

"Are you afraid of losing me?" asks William.

"Sure, I'm afraid of losing you," says Grandma.

"But I'm right here," he says.

"When we get old, we die," says Grandma, "and then I won't be able to see you anymore."

"But if I'm sitting here, will you be able to see me then?"

Grandma thinks for a good while. "Yes, then I'll be able to see you," she says, "even though I'm not here."

"And then you'll be able to see the squirrel, and the white flowers, and the swans, and the magpie too," says William. "Then you can see everything."

"You are absolutely right," says Grandma.

"Now you don't need to be afraid anymore, Grandma." William looks at her.

"No, I don't need to be," she smiles, "when I can see everything I love."

She ruffles William's hair a bit. "Maybe you'll see me too?"

"I guess I will," William says, and smiles back.

Constance Ørbeck-Nilssen studied at the Norwegian Journalist
Academy in Oslo and completed the writing program at the Norwegian
Institute for Children's Books. She now works as a freelance journalist
and children's author, and she has written a number of picture books.
She lives in Norway.

Akin Duzakin is a Turkish-Norwegian illustrator and children's author.
In 2006 he won the Bokkunstprisen award for illustration, and he was
nominated for the Astrid Lindgren Memorial Award in 2007 and 2008.
Akin lives in Norway. Visit his website at www.akinduzakin.com.

First published in the United States in 2015 by
Eerdmans Books for Young Readers,
an imprint of Wm. B. Eerdmans Publishing Co.
2140 Oak Industrial Dr. NE
Grand Rapids, Michigan 49505
P.O. Box 163, Cambridge CB3 9PU U.K.

www.eerdmans.com/youngreaders

Originally published in Norway in 2011
under the title *Jeg er jo her*
by Magikon forlag,
Fjellveien 48 A, Kolbotn, Norway
www.magikon.no
Translation by Jeanne Eirheim

Text © 2011 Constance Ørbeck-Nilssen
Illustrations © 2011 Akin Duzakin
English language translation © 2015 Magikon forlag

Manufactured at Toppan Leefung in China

15 16 17 18 19 20 21 22   1 2 3 4 5 6 7 8 9

FSC
www.fsc.org
MIX
Paper from
responsible sources
FSC® C104723

Library of Congress Cataloging-in-Publication Data

Ørbeck-Nilssen, Constance, 1954-
[Jeg er jo her. English]
I'm right here / by Constance Ørbeck-Nilssen ;
illustrated by Akin Duzakin.
pages cm
Originally published: Kolbotn, Norway : Magikon, 2011,
under the title *Jeg er jo her*.
Summary: Even as William's grandmother soothes him
with the knowledge that his fears will lessen as he grows up,
he reassures her that she need not fear losing the things she
loves.
ISBN 978-0-8028-5455-1
[1. Fear — Fiction. 2. Grandmothers — Fiction. 3. Old age
— Fiction.] I. Duzakin, Akin, 1960- illustrator. II. Title. III.
Title: I'm right here.
PZ7.O762Im 2015
[E] — dc23
2014048101